Footprints in the forest
A Chembakolli story

Taahra Ghazi and Eileen Browne

This book was funded by

DFID Department for
International
Development

It was festival day at last! Kelu pulled on her favourite dress, threw her vanna over her shoulders, tiptoed past Madi, her sleeping sister, and stepped outside.

Dawn was breaking across the blue mountains. The mists hung so low she could hardly see where the trees ended and the sky began.

 She picked up one of her father's sacks and skipped towards the village, smiling as she thought of the special job she had to do.

Kelu had not been up this early since she was very young. Then, her whole family had piled into a cycle rickshaw to go to visit her Aunty Meena in Gudalur.

Kelu remembered clinging to her mother as the driver expertly dodged the buses, trucks and cows which clogged the streets of the busy town.

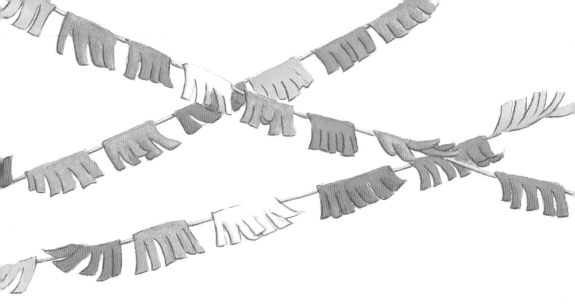

Now everything was early-morning quiet. The village square was a rainbow of decorations which flapped gently in the wind. She stopped to admire them, even though the day before Madi and her friends hadn't let her make any. "Go away!" Madi had snapped. "You're too young to help. You'd just mess things up."

Her mother had found Kelu later, kicking dejectedly at an old tin can. "There's one last job to be done for the festival," she said softly, "if you can get up very early. It's the most important job of all – collecting flowers to put in the Adivasi flag. Remember, it's the flag that shows everyone we are free and proud."

Now Kelu stood alone in the square and gazed up at the flag pole. How tall and still it seemed. Squeezing her eyes shut, she tried to picture what would happen a few hours later.

She heard the drums beating as she watched the Adivasi flag being raised. Then she saw the flowers – her flowers – come tumbling out of it in a mass of golden petals. That would show stuck-up Madi.

"Caw-ah, caw-ah... chick-a-chirr, chick-a-chirr, chick-a-chirr... caw-ah, caw-ah ... tock-tock-tock!" The forest birds sang a hundred different songs as Kelu skipped down the track from the village to the river where the wild flowers grew. She whistled along with them, hoping she'd be able to fill the sack quickly. She didn't want to miss the special festival breakfast her mother was cooking – stuffed parathas!

As she neared the river bank the whistle dried on Kelu's lips. Elephant footprints were everywhere. Beneath them lay hundreds of flowers, their delicate petals trampled into the mud. Kelu looked for the culprit but the elephant had gone. Her eyes filled with tears. How could she go home empty-handed, when the whole village was counting on her? What if they couldn't raise the flag without the flowers?

Then something caught her eye. Leading away from the river was a line of strange tracks. They looked like paw prints, very large paw prints. Kelu knew the tracks of every forest animal, but these she'd never seen before. A cold chill crept up her back as she realised that such unusual footprints could only belong to one animal – puli – the tiger!

Kelu sprang up in surprise. How could a tiger be here, now? Her granny had told her many times how the wild animals had been driven from their forest. "When I was about your age," Granny would say, "the forest belonged to the Adivasi people and to the animals.

"Then one day rich men came and put up fences around the trees. We heard their axes chopping until not a single palm, papaya or jack-fruit tree was left. All the animals, from the biggest black bear to the smallest monkey, fled in panic – all except for one ancient tigress. Night and day she prowled, pining for her lost home. Some say her spirit still returns to drink from the river.

"So, if you see tiger footprints in the forest, Kelu, don't be afraid. The tigress spirit will be watching over you."

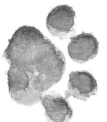

Suddenly Kelu felt brave. She knew her granny was wise. Perhaps the footprints would lead her to another place where wild flowers grew. She knew she must find out.

Up ahead the path began to rise steeply. In some places it was almost worn away but Kelu followed the prints deeper and deeper into the forest. Vines and creepers stroked her face as she pushed her way through the dense undergrowth. The only sounds were the occasional flapping of wings or scurrying of feet as she disturbed small creatures from their hiding places.

This part of the forest was forbidden to Kelu and her sister. Only last week, their father had reminded them never to cross the river.

If he found out, she knew he'd be angry. But if she went back without the flowers, the whole village would be disappointed.

Kelu was so lost in thought, she almost bumped into the fence which blocked the path ahead. Beyond the fence ran the tiger prints; above it loomed a warning sign: PRIVATE LAND. KEEP OUT. Kelu drew a deep breath and squeezed herself through the biggest gap.

On the other side, the trees and vines above Kelu were so thick, they blocked out most of the light. The tiger prints drew her on until she stumbled into a large clearing. Here, the light was so dazzling that she covered her eyes.

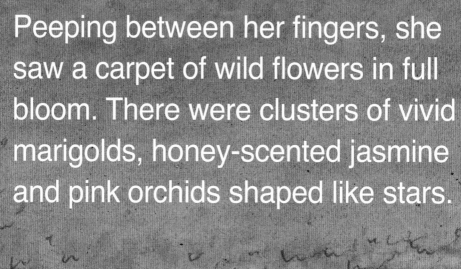

Peeping between her fingers, she saw a carpet of wild flowers in full bloom. There were clusters of vivid marigolds, honey-scented jasmine and pink orchids shaped like stars.

Surrounding the flowers was a
ring of ancient mango trees.
"First food, then work," thought
Kelu. She raced to the trees and
plucked the ripest fruit from
the lower branches.

The sack was almost full of flowers when: "Hoo-ha hoo! Hoo-hoo-ho!" – a tremendous whooping noise froze Kelu to the spot.

She turned round. There, right behind her, was an enormous monkey. It jumped and hooted and snarled with rage. Maybe she'd eaten its breakfast! Kelu grabbed the sack, darted across the clearing and plunged into the forest beyond.

"Hoo-ha hoo-ha hoo. Hoo-ha hoo. Hoo. Ho.o.o.o.o."

The whooping faded as she fought her way through the trees. On and on she struggled until, exhausted, she stumbled over a rock and found herself slithering down a steep, grassy slope. She shut her eyes as she slipped and slid to the bottom. When she opened them, she found herself staring at the feet of a surprised forest worker.

"Kelu!" he cried. "What are you doing here?"

It was Chandran, her father's friend.

"I... I've been collecting these," she panted, out of breath. She held open the sack of flowers to show him. "They're to put in the festival flag. I must get them back in time."

"Don't worry," he smiled, looking down at the beautiful flowers. "We're just about to set off for the festival too."

He called to one of the other men, who was helping an elephant unload its logs: "Let's make sure the flower girl rides home in style!"

Kelu held on tight as the elephant tramped towards the village. It stopped at a pond to drink, dipping its trunk deep into the water. With a huge snort, it sprayed water high into the air. As she watched the spray, Kelu was sure it formed the shape of a tiger. It rose into the sky and then disappeared beyond the clouds.

"Thank you," she whispered. "Thank you for keeping this flower girl safe in the forest."

Later on, Kelu stood again in the village square. She watched with the crowd as the flag was filled with flowers, then hoisted up the pole. As the drums started their deep, rhythmic beat she proudly sang with Madi the festival song:

The Adivasi are coming
From the dark into the light.
We are growing strong
Now our flag is flying.

The crowd was hushed as the flowers fell from the flag. Glinting in the sunlight, they poured down on Kelu and the Adivasi people like a glorious shower of golden rain.

Glossary

vanna: a traditional type of dress made from one piece of cloth, worn by Adivasi women, mainly from the Irula tribe.

paratha: a thin bread originating in India made from flour, water and ghee and often eaten with marsala sauce for breakfast.

puli: meaning tiger in the Irula tribal language.

payasam: a sweet food made with milk, sugar or molasses and either lentils or vermicelli, eaten on special occasions.

Glossary of animals

Bandicoots are similar in size and shape to rabbits and rats. They can be very aggressive and live for a maximum of three years.

Chameleons are lizards known for their ability to change colour. They may be green, yellow or white one minute and brown or black the next. A chameleon's long tongue shoots out so quickly that the human eye can hardly see it.

Giant Squirrels grow up to fifty centimetres long. They are large and fluffy with big eyes and mahogany-red colouring. By jumping off the highest branches of trees, they can fly for 75 metres.

Great Indian Hornbill. Little is known about the Great Indian Hornbill. Its powerful beak is used to pass insects and fruit to its young. A rare and endangered species, it reminds us that much remains to be discovered about bird life in the rain forest.

Ground Squirrels have stout bodies with short, dense fur. Flowers, seeds, fruit and bulbs form the bulk of their diet. Their days are spent looking for food, before they retreat to their burrows at night.

Hanuman Langur Monkey is a handsome, long-tailed, leaf-eating monkey. Its hair forms a crest around its head, similar to a fur coat.

Kingfishers have large heads, small tails and a brilliant blue-green plumage. They sit motionless on waterside branches watching their prey, and then plunge headlong into the water with their long spear-like bills.

Lion-tailed Macaque Monkey. The Latin name for this species is Macaca Silenus. They are extremely rare and roam widely in the forest. Sounding a loud "hoo", they pounce on their prey, which include fast-moving lizards and giant, walking stick insects.

The Red Tailed Cockatoo is a parrot with a crest of light coloured feathers around its head. Its vivid red tail can be seen in the dense canopies of the rain forest.

Tree Frog. Despite their small size, tree frogs can leap enormous distances. Suction pads on their toes help them to grip branches and leaves. They feed on insects by jumping up and catching them with their long tongues.

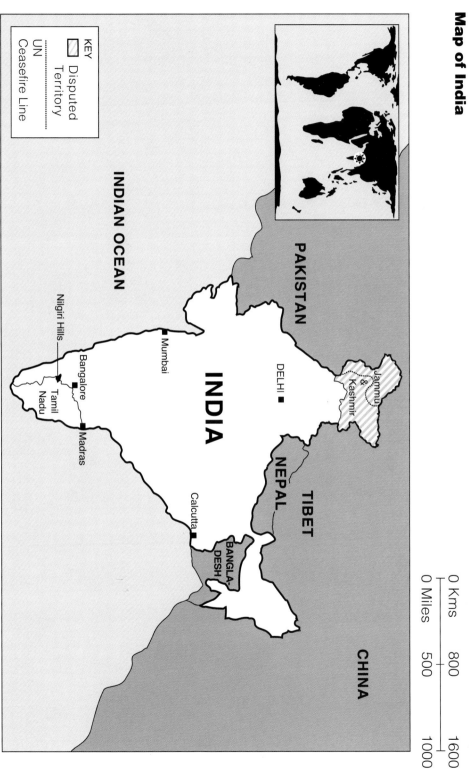

KEY

Disputed
Territory

UN
Ceasefire Line

INDIAN OCEAN

Nilgiri Hills

Mumbai

Bangalore

Tamil
Nadu

Madras

DELHI

INDIA

Jammu
&
Kashmir

PAKISTAN

NEPAL

TIBET

Calcutta

BANGLA-
DESH

CHINA

0 Kms   800   1600
0 Miles   500   1000

Map of the Nilgiri District

N
W — E
S

Karnataka

Kerala

Mudumalai
Wild Life
Sanctuary

Chembakolli

Kanjikolly

Nilgiri Hills
(Tamil Nadu)

Gudalur

Ootacamund

Coonoor

Kerala

Coimbatore District
(Tamil Nadu)

Key

——— Nilgiri District
boundary

------- State boundary

▓▓▓ Road

■ Town

● Village

0   5   10 Km